Little Sister

Caryn Pearson

Karen's Dinosaur
Ann M. Martin

Illustrations by Susan Tang

A
LITTLE APPLE
PAPERBACK

SC...
New York Toront...

This book is for
Nora Godwin Allen

No part of this publication may be reproduced in whole or in part, or stored in a retrieval system, or transmitted in any form or by any means, electronic, mechanical, photocopying, recording, or otherwise, without written permission of the publisher. For information regarding permission, write to Scholastic Inc., 555 Broadway, New York, NY 10012.

ISBN 0-590-26301-3

Copyright © 1996 by Ann M. Martin. All rights reserved. Published by Scholastic Inc. BABY-SITTER'S LITTLE SISTER, APPLE PAPERBACKS, and the APPLE PAPERBACKS logo are registered trademarks of Scholastic Inc.

12 11 10 9 8 7 6 5 4 3 2 1   6 7 8 9/9 0 1/0

Printed in the U.S.A.   40

First Scholastic printing, May 1996

Waiting for the Bus

Stegosaurus. Tyrannosaurus. Diplodocus. Allosaurus. Apatosaurus. I was thinking about dinosaurs as I stood at the school bus stop. I was waiting for the bus. I was also waiting for my best friend, Hannie Papadakis. Actually, Hannie is one of my two best friends. The other one is Nancy Dawes. Hannie and Nancy and I call ourselves the Three Musketeers. We are in Ms. Colman's second-grade class at Stoneybrook Academy here in Stoneybrook, Connecticut. And we are studying dinosaurs.

I am Karen Brewer. I am seven years old. So are Nancy and Hannie. I have long blonde hair, blue eyes, and some freckles. I wear glasses. I even have two pairs. The blue pair is for reading. The pink pair is for the rest of the time.

"Hi, Karen!" Hannie called. She was running across the street toward the bus stop. She was carrying a big book.

"What is that?" I asked.

Hannie held it out to me. "It is about dinosaurs," she replied. "I took it out of the library yesterday. Look at this."

Hannie opened the book. I saw rows of pictures of dinosaurs. Under each picture was the dinosaur's name.

"Wow. Some of these names are hard to say." I peered at them. I tried to sound them out. The first one was pachycephalosaurus. "Pack-ee-cef-a-la-sor-us," I said slowly. The next one was dromiceiomimus. "Drom — drom — " I could not say that one at all.

"We will have to ask Mrs. Hoffman about it," said Hannie.

Mrs. Hoffman is our substitute teacher. She has been our substitute teacher for quite awhile. That is because Ms. Colman just had a baby. Ms. Colman will come back to school in June. (It is May now.) Mrs. Hoffman is the one who has been teaching our class about dinosaurs.

"Hey, what is David Michael doing?" asked Hannie.

David Michael is my stepbrother. He goes to a different school, Stoneybrook Elementary. (He is in second grade, just like I am.) He waits at a different bus stop. It is farther down the sidewalk from ours. Usually, David Michael fools around with the other kids at his bus stop. But that morning, he was sitting on a big rock. He kept turning the pages of a book, then writing in a workbook.

"He must be finishing his homework," said Hannie.

"No. Last night he said he did not have any homework." I frowned. Then I yelled, "Hey, David Michael, what are you doing?"

"None of your business!" he yelled back, which was very rude.

"It is homework, isn't it?"

"I *said*, none of your business!"

"What a grouch," I said to Hannie. "He is probably mad because he had homework last night and he forgot about it. The same thing happened on Tuesday."

Hannie opened the dinosaur book again. "Well, anyway," she said, "here is a dinosaur called di — dinon — Hmm. I am not sure what it is called. But its name means 'terrible claw.' Isn't that cool?"

"Let me see it," I said. I could not pronounce its name either. But the picture of deinonychus looked quite fierce.

Our bus arrived then. I took one last look at David Michael sitting on that rock, trying to finish his homework. Then I scrambled onto the bus after Hannie.

Hannie and I used to be afraid of the big kids on the bus, but we are not anymore. We opened Hannie's book and looked at the dinosaurs again. We looked at them as the bus lurched its way to Stoneybrook Academy.

Mrs. Hoffman

When the bus stopped in the school parking lot, Hannie snapped her book shut. We hopped off the bus. We ran to the front door of our school. Then we walked to our classroom. (We are not allowed to run in the halls.)

"Good morning, Hannie. Good morning, Karen," said Mrs. Hoffman.

"Good morning," we replied.

Guess what. When I first met Mrs. Hoffman, I did not like her. In fact, I hated her. So I called her Hatey Hoffman. But that did not last long. Now my classmates and I understand Mrs. Hoffman, and she understands us. She is our favorite substitute teacher ever.

Hannie and I put our things away in our cubbies. Then we went to the back of the room to wait for Nancy Dawes. Hannie and Nancy sit together in the back row. I used to sit with them. That was before I got my glasses. When I got my glasses, Ms. Colman moved me to the front row with the other glasses-wearers. She thinks I can see the board better from there. Ms. Colman ought to know. She is a glasses-wearer herself.

While we waited for Nancy, I watched my classmates enter the room. I saw Ricky Torres and Natalie Springer. They are the other glasses-wearers. I saw Terri and Tammy Barkan, the twins. I saw Sara Ford, who was new this year. I saw Addie Sidney in her wheelchair. She was new this year, too. I saw Pamela Harding, Jannie Gilbert, and Leslie Morris. They are best friends, but I call them my best enemies. I saw Omar Harris and Chris Lamar, Audrey Green and Hank Reubens, and Bobby Gianelli and Ian Johnson. Eighteen kids in all.

Nancy was the last one to arrive. I looked at the clock. Goody. Five more minutes until the bell would ring. We had a little time to play with Hootie and Evelyn. They are our class guinea pigs. Hootie and Evelyn live in separate cages. That is because Hootie is a boy and Evelyn is a girl. They used to live in the same cage, but then Evelyn had babies. That was fun, but Ms. Colman said we could only let it happen once.

Hootie and Evelyn were still scurrying around on the floor when the bell rang.

"Okay, class!" called Mrs. Hoffman.

We put the guinea pigs in their cages.

My classmates and I hurried to our seats. " 'Bye, you guys," I said to Nancy and Hannie. "See you at lunchtime." I sat down. My desk faces our teacher's desk. It is smack in front of it. That is so our teacher can keep her eye on me. In case I get out of hand. (I have a little trouble remembering to raise my hand. Also a little trouble settling down.)

I sit between Ricky Torres and Natalie Springer. Ricky is my pretend husband. We got married on the playground one day. Natalie is nice, but her socks are always falling down.

"Natalie," said Mrs. Hoffman, "would you take attendance today?"

Mrs. Hoffman handed the roll book to Natalie. Natalie took it proudly. Then she made a check mark for each person who had come to school that day. Since no one was absent, she made eighteen marks. She handed the book back to Mrs. Hoffman.

"Thank you," said Mrs. Hoffman. "Now, how many of you will be buying lunch in the cafeteria today?"

Nine people raised their hands.

"And how many of you still need to talk to me about the after-school clubs?"

Four people raised their hands.

"Okay," Mrs. Hoffman went on. "Let me

see. Jannie and Ian, you need to hand in your reading worksheets."

"Here is mine!" called Jannie.

"And mine!" called Ian.

"Thank you. And now," said Mrs. Hoffman, "I have an announcement to make."

Class Trip

Mrs. Hoffman was going to make an announcement. Hmm. Whenever Ms. Colman makes an announcement, I get very excited. She usually makes Surprising Announcements. They are about good things. She might tell us we are going to put on a play. Or begin an art project. Or plant a garden of our own. Once she told us we were going to adopt grandparents. Then there was the time she told us she was going to have a baby.

I wondered if Mrs. Hoffman's announcement would be as wonderful as Ms. Colman's Surprising Announcements.

It was.

"Girls and boys," began Mrs. Hoffman, "we have, as you know, just begun learning about dinosaurs. In the next few weeks we will learn lots of things about them. Then, at the end of our unit, we will take a field trip."

"Yea!" I cried.

"A field trip to where?" asked Bobby.

Mrs. Hoffman smiled. "A field trip to New York City."

"To New York *City*?" repeated Sara. "Cool."

"Very cool," added Pamela.

I turned around and grinned at Nancy and Hannie. They grinned back.

"Why are we going to New York?" asked Omar.

"Good question," said Mrs. Hoffman. "We are going to New York to visit the American Museum of Natural History. It is a wonderful place. At the museum you can learn about nature, animals, rocks and minerals, history, people, and lots more."

"Can you learn about dinosaurs?" I asked.

"You certainly can. On the fourth floor are the dinosaur halls. You will find displays, things to touch, computers you can talk to, fossils, and even dinosaur skeletons."

"*Skeletons?*" cried Ricky.

"Of whole dinosaurs?" asked Tammy.

"Yup," said Mrs. Hoffman.

"Is there an apatosaurus?" asked Chris.

"I believe so," replied Mrs. Hoffman.

We were so excited that Mrs. Hoffman had to ask us to settle down, please. Then she said something that was so surprising and wonderful I could not believe it.

"Guess who will be going with us to the museum."

"The room parents?" suggested Natalie.

"Well, yes. But also . . . your pen pals in Miss Mandel's class."

This was too much for me. I leaped out

of my seat. "I will get to see Maxie again!" I cried.

"Indoor voice, Karen," said Mrs. Hoffman.

Everyone in our class has a pen pal in a second-grade classroom in New York City. Our pen pals' teacher is Miss Mandel. She is a friend of Ms. Colman's. We write letters to our pen pals, and once they visited our school here in Stoneybrook. My pen pal is named Maxie Medvin. She lives in an apartment in the city. She is already eight years old. She has older sisters who are twins, and younger brothers who are adopted. Maxie and I are very good friends. I was glad we would get to see each other again.

"On the day of our trip," Mrs. Hoffman said, "the bus will take us to your pen pals' school. You will meet your friends and see their classroom. Then, together, we will walk to Central Park for a picnic lunch. After that, we will go to the museum where each of you will work on a dinosaur project with your pen pal. Your pen pals have been learning about dinosaurs, too. I am not going to tell you much about the project yet. For now, all you need to know is that you and your pen pal must choose a dinosaur ahead of time. So keep your eyes open for a dinosaur you especially like or think is interesting."

"Excuse me, Mrs. Hoffman?" said Addie. "I have a problem."

"What is it?"

"I do not have a pen pal."

Two by Two

It turned out that Addie did not have a problem after all.

"I know you joined our class after your friends met their pen pals," said Mrs. Hoffman. "But guess what. Miss Mandel's class has a new student, too. His name is Jamal, and he will be your pen pal."

Addie smiled. And that was the end of her problem.

That afternoon, Hannie and I bounced home together on the rattly schoolbus. I was still excited about our field trip. I could not wait to tell my two families about it.

Why do I have two families? Well, it is like this:

A long time ago, when I was still in preschool, I lived with one family. Mommy, Daddy, Andrew, and me. (Andrew is my little brother. He is four going on five now.) We lived in a big house here in Stoneybrook. I thought Mommy and Daddy were happy, but I guess they were not. They decided to get a divorce. They said they loved Andrew and me very much, but they did not love each other anymore.

After the divorce, Mommy moved to a little house. Daddy stayed nearby in the big house. (It is the house he grew up in.) Later, Mommy and Daddy each got married again. Mommy married Seth. He is my stepfather. Daddy married Elizabeth. She is my stepmother.

So now Andrew and I have two families. Every other month we live with Daddy at the big house. During the in-between months we live with Mommy at the little house. These are the people and pets in each of my families:

In my little-house family are Mommy, Seth, Andrew, me, Rocky, Midgie, Emily Junior, and Bob. Rocky and Midgie are Seth's cat and dog. Emily Junior is my pet rat. Bob is Andrew's hermit crab.

In my big-house family are Daddy, Elizabeth, Kristy, Sam, Charlie, David Michael, Emily Michelle, Nannie, Andrew, me, Shannon, Boo-Boo, Crystal Light the Second, Goldfishie, Emily Junior, and Bob. (Emily Junior and Bob go back and forth with Andrew and me.) Kristy, Sam, Charlie, and David Michael are Elizabeth's kids, so they are my stepsister and stepbrothers. (Elizabeth was married once before she married Daddy.) Kristy is thirteen, and one of my favorite people in the world. Sam and Charlie are old. They go to high school. And as you know, David Michael is seven like me. Emily Michelle is two and a half. Daddy and Elizabeth adopted her from the faraway country of Vietnam. I love Emily. That is why I named my special pet rat after her. Nannie is Elizabeth's mother. That makes her my stepgrandmother. Nannie helps take care of the house and all us kids.

Shannon is not a person. She is one of the pets. She is David Michael's big, floppy puppy. Boo-Boo is Daddy's fat old cat. (Sometimes he hisses and scratches.) Crystal Light is my goldfish. And Goldfishie is Andrew's you-know-what.

I made up nicknames for my brother and me. I call us Andrew Two-Two and Karen Two-Two. I thought up those names after Ms. Colman read a very wonderful book to our class. It was called *Jacob Two-Two Meets the Hooded Fang*. We are two-twos because we have two of so many things. We have two houses and two families, two mommies and two daddies, two cats and two dogs. I have two stuffed cats named Goosie and Moosie. Goosie stays at the little house, Moosie stays at the big house. I have two bicycles and Andrew has two tricycles. In fact, we each have toys and books and clothes at both houses. That is so we do not have to pack much when we go back and forth.

Do you know what else I have two of? Glasses (I already told you that). And best friends. Nancy lives next door to the little house. Hannie lives across the street from Daddy's and one house down.

Sometimes being a two-two is confusing. But mostly it is fine. I like it. I am lucky to have two families who love me.

Dinosaur Skeletons

When the bus pulled up to our stop, Hannie and I hopped down the steps.

"See you later!" I called to Hannie.

I ran to the big house. I opened the front door. "Hello!" I called.

"Hello!" replied Nannie and Andrew. I found them in the kitchen. They were fixing snacks. Emily was there, too. She was sitting in her high chair. But she did not say anything. She was sleepy because she had just woken up from her nap.

"Guess what!" I exclaimed.

"What?" said Nannie and Andrew.

"When we finish learning about dinosaurs, we are going to go to the American Museum of Natural History in New York City."

"In New *York*?!" cried Andrew.

"Really?" said Nannie. "That is wonderful. How exciting."

"Remember when we went to New York?" said Andrew.

"Yup," I replied. "That was fun." Last December, Mommy and Seth and Andrew and I went to New York for a whole weekend. We even visited Maxie at her apartment.

"Why are you going to the museum?" Andrew wanted to know.

"To see the dinosaurs."

"*Real* dinosaurs?"

"No, silly. Dinosaur skeletons."

"Ew," said Andrew.

"Nannie? Can I tell Daddy my news?" I asked. Daddy works at home. His office is right here in the big house. But we are not supposed to disturb him unless it is Very Important.

"I guess so," said Nannie. "But be quick. No chattering." (Sometimes I talk a little too much.)

I knocked on the door to Daddy's office. I told him the news.

"Fantastic!" he said.

Then I heard David Michael come home. I closed Daddy's door and ran back to the kitchen.

"David Michael! Guess what," I said. "We are studying dinosaurs with Mrs. Hoffman and in a few weeks we are going to go on a field trip. We are going to New York City to the American Museum of Natural History to see the dinosaur skeletons. We will work on a project there."

David Michael did not look as happy as everyone else had looked. He narrowed his eyes at me. "You are?"

"Yup."

"*We* are learning about dinosaurs, too," said David Michael. "And our teacher did not say anything about going to New York or a museum."

"Well — " I started to say.

"But she did say," David Michael went on, "that we are going to have a project at the end of our unit. Maybe we will do our project in the museum. Just like you are going to do." David Michael was smiling. He loves dinosaurs. And he would especially love a trip to the dinosaur halls.

"Did your teacher *say* you are going to take a trip?" I asked.

"No," replied David Michael. "She must be planning a surprise."

"I don't know. That sounds — "

"Never mind," said David Michael. "I know it is a surprise."

That night, I did my homework at the kitchen table. David Michael sat across from me with a worksheet. My homework was about dinosaur footprints. David Michael's was about subtraction.

David Michael filled in the answers fast.

25

He wrote big messy numbers and he made lots of mistakes. He did not check his work.

I looked at pictures of dinosaur footprints. I was supposed to decide which dinosaur had made them. Then I drew a line from the footprints to a picture of the dinosaur.

That night I dreamed about a diplodocus named Daisy.

The Dinosaur Hall
of Fame

One day Mrs. Hoffman said, "Girls and boys, today each of you is going to make a Dinosaur Hall of Fame."

"A hall of fame?" said Audrey. "What is that?"

"Who knows what a hall of fame is?" Mrs. Hoffman asked us.

"Is it like a museum?" asked Hank.

"It is about famous people," said Addie.

"And records they set," added Hannie.

Mrs. Hoffman smiled. "In your halls of fame, you are going to put record-setting dinosaurs. The biggest, the fastest, the longest, and any other records you can think of. You can look up dinosaurs in these books I checked out of our library. And on these sheets you can draw their pictures and fill in the records they set. When you are finished, you will each have a Dinosaur Hall of Fame. While you are working, you can keep your eyes out for a dinosaur to choose for your museum project."

Mrs. Hoffman handed out the sheets and we set to work. I found a book called *Dinosaurs and How They Lived*. I found some other good books, too. The first thing I wanted to know was which dinosaurs were the biggest. Was tyrannosaurus one of the biggest? Yes, but brachiosaurus weighed about 77 tons, which is about 154 *thousand* pounds. I drew a picture of brachiosaurus inside a frame on the worksheet. Under that I spelled out B-R-A-C-H-I-O-S-A-U-R-U-S. Under that I wrote: Heaviest — 77 tons.

The longest dinosaur was diplodocus. It

was about 88 feet long. Its tail was 46 feet long.

The tallest dinosaur was barosaurus. It could reach as high as a five-story building. Its neck was more than 30 feet long.

The dinosaur with the longest neck was mamenchisaurus. *Its* neck was 50 feet long, which is the longest of any animal ever. (That is as long as three giraffe necks.)

The smallest dinosaur was saltopus. It was only two feet long, not much bigger than Boo-Boo.

I filled in lots of dinosaurs in my hall of fame. I wondered if I should choose one of them for my project with Maxie. I sort of liked the little tiny dinosaurs. But I liked the huge ones, too. And the heavy ones. And the ones with the long necks.

I wondered which ones Maxie liked.

Wanted!

Our class had been learning about dinosaurs for almost two weeks. Our halls of fame were finished. Mrs. Hoffman had spread them out on a table at the back of the room. We could look at them whenever we wanted. Guess what. We found that we did not agree on everything.

Jannie found a book that said compsognathus was the smallest dinosaur. I had found a book that said saltopus was the smallest.

Ian found a book that said barosaurus

was the biggest dinosaur. I had found a book that said barosaurus was the *tallest*. But I could not even find barosaurus in some other books.

"Dinosaurs are hard to study," said Mrs. Hoffman."They lived millions and millions of years ago. We have found fossils of dinosaur teeth and bones. But they are only clues about what dinosaurs were really like. We have to make some guesses. That is one reason dinosaurs are so interesting."

Mrs. Hoffman paused. Then she said, "Class, it is time for me to tell you about the project you will work on in the museum with your pen pals. I think you will have fun with this project and learn something, too. At the museum, you will make a wanted poster about the dinosaur you have chosen. It will look like the wanted poster for a criminal."

Ricky raised his hand. "I saw a cartoon once, and this cat who was the sheriff of a town put up a wanted poster in the post office. It was a poster of a dog, and the dog had robbed the bank."

Mrs. Hoffman smiled. "Do you remember what the poster said?"

"It said 'WANTED: Wild Dawg Mc-Cready. For bank robbery.' And then it said what Wild Dawg looked like. Oh, and there was a picture of him."

My classmates and I giggled.

Mrs. Hoffman said, "Exactly. That is just what you are going to do for your dinosaur. You must know a lot about your dinosaur to be able to make the poster. You must know what your dinosaur looked like, so you can draw it and describe it. You must know what its habits were, so you can write down what it is wanted for." Mrs. Hoffman held up a piece of paper. "I made my own wanted poster last night," she said, "so I can show you a sample. This one is for styracosaurus."

I looked at the poster. Underneath Mrs. Hoffman's drawing of the dinosaur, she had printed "WANTED: Styracosaurus. For fierce horn attack. Appearance: 18 feet long, walks on all fours, bony nose horn, six spikes around frill."

It was a very cool poster.

Omar raised his hand. "Mrs. Hoffman?" he said. "How will my pen pal and I choose a dinosaur?"

"Good question," said Mrs. Hoffman. "You are going to write to your pen pals. I know you have been thinking about dinosaurs for your project, and so have your pen pals. Now each of you is going to write a letter, and list three dinosaurs you like. Your pen pal will choose one dinosaur from your list and write back to you with his choice."

I was glad I had been looking at so many dinosaurs lately. I knew just which three dinosaurs to suggest to Maxie. At least, I thought I did. I flipped through Hannie's book one more time. Then I began my letter to my pen pal.

DEAR MAXIE,

I HAVE LOOKED AT LOTS AND LOTS OF DINOSAURS. I LIKE THREE OF THEM VERY MUCH. ONE IS ORNITHOLESTES. SOME BOOKS CALL IT A BIRD ROBBER! THEN I LIKE MAMENCHISAURUS WITH THE LONG, LONG NECK. AND THEN I LIKE PENTACERATOPS WITH ITS HORN AND FRILL. WHICH ONE DO YOU LIKE? I CANNOT WAIT TO SEE YOU AND VISIT YOUR SCHOOL!

LOVE,
KAREN

Ornitholestes

I waited and waited for my letter from Maxie. I had to wait for a whole week. I was sort of hoping Maxie would choose pentaceratops. Guess what "penta" means. It means "five." And guess how many horns are on pentaceratops's head. Five. Isn't that cool? That is what I like about pentaceratops. I liked the other dinosaurs, too, though.

One morning, a week later, Mrs. Hoffman held up a fat brown envelope. "I have letters for you from your pen pals," she said.

"Oh, goody!" I exclaimed.

"Indoor voice, Karen," said Mrs. Hoffman.

Mrs. Hoffman let Pamela hand out the letters.

This is what my letter said:

Dear Karen,

Hi! It is me, Maxie! I got your letter and I like all those dinosaurs. Well, actually. I do not like mamenchisaurus very much. Its neck is way too long. So I did not choose mamenchisaurus. And I like pentaceratops, but I did not choose that one either. I chose ornitholestes. I like ornitholestes because it was little (for a dinosaur), but fast. And it was naughty! They think it might have eaten baby dinosaurs, too. Ew, ew, ew! I cannot wait to see you either.

Love ya!
Maxie

Well, ornitholestes had not been my first choice. But I liked what Maxie said about it. She made ornitholestes sound funny. So I was happy with the dinosaur for our project.

When I returned home from school that day, I ran into the kitchen.

"Guess what — " I started to say. Then I stopped. David Michael was already at home. He was talking to Nannie and Andrew. I took a good look at his face. "What is wrong?" I asked.

David Michael scowled at me. "Our teacher told us what our special project is going to be. We get to pick any dinosaur we want and write a report on it. A report. Whoopee. Big deal."

"Gee," I said. "No field trip? No museum?"

"Nope. Just a stupid report." David Michael scowled harder. "Don't you think that was no fair?" he said to Nannie. "Special project. That is exactly what Ms. Fairmont said. *Special* project. She is so mean. Plus, she gives us way too much homework. And she gives my papers back to me with red marks all over them. They look like they have poison ivy."

Andrew giggled. But David Michael was not trying to be funny. He stuck his tongue out at Andrew. Then he pouted.

I wanted to make him feel better. "Did you choose your dinosaur yet?" I asked him. "At least you could choose a really good one."

David Michael actually smiled. "Yup," he said proudly. "I chose my favorite of all. Ornitholestes."

"Hey, cool!" I exclaimed. "That is the dinosaur I chose for *my* project! See, when we get to the museum, Maxie and I are supposed to make a wanted poster for our dinosaur. We have to know a lot about ornitholestes to do that. We have to know what it looked like and — "

"And you chose ornitholestes? Same as *me*?" David Michael cried. "Why did you have to go and do that? *I* chose ornitho-lestes. It is *my* dinosaur. And I do not even get to go on a trip or anything. Why should you get a trip, and my dinosaur, too? No fair."

Uh-oh.

Greedy Guts

I left David Michael alone for awhile. I stomped upstairs to our playroom. I talked to Crystal Light and Goldfishie. (Their tank is in the playroom.) I told them David Michael was being unreasonable.

"Do you know what that means?" I asked Crystal Light. "It means he is being silly and not thinking things through. He needs to calm down and quiet down and settle down."

"I do not."

Oops. David Michael was standing in the doorway.

"I do not need to calm down and quiet down and settle down," he said. "And I am not being unreasonable."

"Okay, okay," I replied.

"But you are being a greedy guts," David Michael went on.

"A greedy guts?!" I exclaimed. "Me?"

"Yes, you." David Michael put his hands on his hips.

"Am not!"

"Are too. You always get everything you want. You got a pony — "

"An old, falling-apart pony I could not ride. And I do not even have it anymore. We gave it away."

"And you got to be the Pizza Queen — "

"I won a contest. I won it fair and square."

"And you got a new bike — "

"I had to pay for part of it with my own money."

"And you always get A's in school."

"I cannot help it. I am very — " I paused. I had started to say, "I am very smart." Instead I said, "I mean, I like school."

"And you have two of almost everything."

"I cannot help that, either. I live at two different places."

"And now," David Michael went on. (He was ignoring everything I said.) "And now you get to go on a trip to New York City. And you get to see the dinosaur skeletons. *And* you chose my dinosaur."

Well, for heaven's sake. How was I supposed to know David Michael would choose ornitholestes for his report? I did not even know he was going to have to write a report.

"Maybe you could choose a different dinosaur," I suggested. "We do not have to have the same one. How about pentaceratops? That is one of my favorites. It has five horns. Or dimetrodon. Or — "

"I do not want another dinosaur!" cried

David Michael. "I already told Ms. Fairmont I chose ornitholestes. I do not want to talk to her again and tell her I changed my mind." (I had a feeling David Michael might be in trouble with Ms. Fairmont.) "Besides, I *like* ornitholestes. It is my favorite dinosaur. Why don't you change *your* dinosaur?"

"Me?!" I exclaimed. "No way. Maxie and I agreed on ornitholestes. I had to write a letter to her, and she had to write one back to me. It would take forever to choose another one. Besides, we like ornitholestes, too."

"See what I mean, you greedy guts?" said David Michael. "You get everything you want." He paused. "And you *do* everything you want."

"I do not!" I shouted. "I cannot help that Mrs. Hoffman decided to take us to the museum. And I cannot help that Maxie and I like ornitholestes, too."

"I don't care. You are still a greedy guts."

"You are a stupey-dupe!"

"Barf-face!"

"Baby!"

David Michael ran to his room. He slammed his door.

So I ran to my room and slammed my door.

Butterflies

My classmates and I had been learning about dinosaurs for a long time. We knew which ones were plant-eaters and which ones were meat-eaters. We knew that at the museum there are two dinosaur halls. The dinosaurs in one hall are saurischians. The dinosaurs in the other hall are ornithischians. The saurischians had grasping hands and were "lizard-hipped." Their hip bones were shaped like lizards'. The ornithischians were "bird-hipped." Their hip bones were shaped like birds'.

I was ready for our trip to New York. I was ready to see the skeletons and fossils and displays. I was ready to make a wanted poster for my dinosaur. So I was very happy that it was now the night before our field trip. The very next day I would go to the American Museum of Natural History. And I would see Maxie again.

I was so excited I had butterflies in my stomach.

I was excited even though David Michael was still mad at me.

Guess what. David Michael was *so* mad that he would hardly speak to me. He spoke to me only when he really needed something. Otherwise, he ignored me. Sometimes he even turned his head away.

On the night before our trip, I had to do lots of things. I packed my lunch for our picnic in Central Park.

"Be sure you pack things that will keep until lunchtime," said Elizabeth. "No mayonnaise or eggs."

This is what I packed: a peanut butter and jam sandwich, an apple, some carrot sticks, and for a treat, two chocolate lollipops. (One was for Maxie.) Elizabeth said she would give me a cold pack from the freezer the next day, to be sure everything stayed fresh and cool.

"Is this a healthy lunch?" I asked Elizabeth.

"Pretty healthy," she replied. "The jam and the chocolate are sugary. But the other things are good. You even chose whole wheat bread." (I try to eat healthy foods, but I do like sugar. I cannot help it.)

When my lunch was ready, I put the bag in the refrigerator. Then I thought about what I was going to wear the next day. I wanted to wear fancy party clothes. I wanted to look nice at Maxie's school and in the museum. But I did not think a dress and my shiny Mary Jane shoes would be the best clothes for a picnic in the park. I looked in my closet for a long time. Then

I looked in my dresser drawers. Finally I chose a pair of blue jeans. Then I chose my underwear and my sneakers.

"Now, which top?" I asked myself.

I pulled out three. One was the Stoneybrook High School sweatshirt Charlie had given me. One had a picture of New York City on the front. Another had a picture of a cat's face on the front and a cat's tail on the back. I liked all of the tops very much. At last I decided to wear the New York shirt. What better place to wear it than in New York?

After I laid out my clothes, I pulled a box out of my desk drawer. The box was full of beads, and it was a present for Maxie. I thought my pen pal would have fun making necklaces and bracelets. Mrs. Hoffman had not told us to bring presents for our pen pals, but I wanted to do something nice for Maxie.

I laid the bead box on my bed. I wrapped it in dinosaur paper.

David Michael walked by my room. He

saw the present. He saw the dinosaur paper. But he did not say anything. He just stuck out his tongue.

I stuck mine out at him. "Baby!" I called.

"Dinosaur stealer!" he shouted back.

"Choose another dinosaur!" I said.

"Why don't you?"

I sighed. I told myself to forget about David Michael and think about the trip.

The Best Bus

The next morning, my alarm clock rang at six o'clock.

"Six o'clock!" I cried. "What is wrong with this clock? It is not supposed to ring until — " I stopped. I remembered something.

"The trip!" I exclaimed. "Today is New York! Today is the museum! Today is Maxie! Today is ornitholestes!"

I leaped out of bed. I flicked on the light. Then I put on the outfit I had chosen the night before. I looked at myself in the mirror. I was ready for a trip to New York City all right.

I hurried downstairs. I was up very early, but Nannie and Daddy were up, too. Daddy was going to drive Hannie and me to school. Our bus was going to leave at 7:45. That is before our school is even open.

"Good morning," I said as I sat down at the kitchen table.

"Good morning," replied Daddy.

"Ready for your trip?" asked Nannie.

"Yup." I pointed to my shirt.

"Ah. New York. Good choice," said Daddy.

After breakfast, I put Maxie's present in my backpack. Then I slipped my backpack on. I took my lunch out of the fridge. Then I took the cold pack out of the freezer and put it in my lunch bag to keep the food cool.

"Do you have everything you need?" Elizabeth asked. She yawned.

"I think so. Lunch, jacket, games to play

on the bus, my spending money, present for Maxie."

"Good girl," said Elizabeth.

"Daddy, can we go now? Puh-*lease*?" I asked. "I cannot wait a moment longer." I was hopping from one foot to the other.

Daddy looked at his watch. "It is a little early, but I guess so. Do you think Hannie is ready?"

I peeked out the front door. "She is standing on her porch!" I cried.

"Okay," said Daddy. "Wagons ho."

Daddy drove Hannie and me to school. In the parking lot was a huge bus. It was not a yellow school bus. It said *Charter Tours* on the side. Mrs. Hoffman was standing next to it, talking to the driver. Nearby were Addie and her mom, Sara and her dad, and Nancy and her dad. Mrs. Sidney, Mr. Ford, and Mr. Dawes were coming along on the trip. They were going to be our room parents.

"Ooh, look at the bus! This is so exciting!" I said to Hannie.

Daddy parked the car, and Hannie and I hopped out. We ran to join our friends. "Hi! Here we are!" called Hannie.

Daddy stayed to talk to Mr. Dawes.

By seven-thirty, all of my classmates had arrived. The driver opened the door of the wonderful bus.

"You can go now," I whispered to Daddy.

Daddy nodded. "Pay attention to Mrs. Hoffman," he told me. "And to the parents. Do everything they tell you to do. Follow Mrs. Hoffman's trip rules. And be very, *very* careful crossing the streets in New York. Promise?"

"Promise," I said. Then I added, "Daddy? Please don't kiss me good-bye, okay? Everyone would see."

"Okay," said Daddy. "Have fun, Karen!" He climbed into his car and drove away.

My friends and I found our trip partners and climbed onto the bus. My trip partner was Hannie. (Well, she was my trip partner until we reached New York. Then Maxie would be my partner.) Hannie and I sat near the front of the bus. Nancy and Audrey sat behind us.

When we had settled down, Mrs. Hoffman said, "Boys and girls, remember the trip rules we have been talking about. Especially remember what to do if you get lost. Find a police officer or an adult you can trust. Do not wander away by yourself. Stay where you are, and I will find you as fast as I can. And now . . . have fun! By the way, there is a bathroom at the back of the bus."

"A bathroom?" Hannie said to me. "Wow, this is the best bus ever!"

Skyscrapers

Hannie and I sat back in our seats. The bus ride was going to be more than two hours long. But we had brought plenty of things to do.

"Let's play cat's cradle first," said Hannie.

So we did. We made string figures as Stoneybrook slipped by outside the windows of the bus. Then we played the license plate game with Nancy and Audrey. We had left Stoneybrook, and we were riding down the highway. We should have seen lots of different plates. But . . .

"This is boring," complained Audrey. "All we see are license plates from Connecticut and New York. I want to see something good. Like something from Canada."

But we did not.

So Hannie pulled out her magnetic checkers game. She and I played two games. Then I took a little nap. Well, actually it was a big nap. The next thing I knew, Hannie was tugging at me.

"I think we are almost there!" she said.

I blinked my eyes. I looked out the window. We were still flying down the highway. But in the distance I could see a group of tall buildings.

"Look! Skyscrapers!" I exclaimed.

"A bridge!" added Hannie.

"Boys and girls, we have almost reached New York City," announced Mrs. Hoffman. She was standing near the driver. "Very soon we will arrive at your pen pals'

school," she added. Then she sat down again.

The driver turned onto a smaller highway. A little while later, he turned off the highway, and I saw that we were driving through city streets. Block after block went by. The streets were lined with stores and apartment buildings and schools. I looked at the street signs. Now we were traveling down a street called Central Park West. We passed 91st Street, then 90th, then 89th, 88th . . . a few blocks later, our driver slowed down. He turned right. I saw that we were on a quiet street. Most of the buildings were just a few stories high. They looked like a row of little houses. The driver pulled up in front of one of the buildings. A sign by the door said Park West School.

"Here we are!" called Mrs. Hoffman.

Hello, Maxie!

Mrs. Hoffman stood at the front of the bus. "Okay, class," she said. "Please stay with your partners until we reach Miss Mandel's room. Remember our trip rules. Also remember that Park West is a school like any other, so please follow our school rules here, too."

"Hello?" called a man. He was waiting on the steps to Park West. "Are you Mrs. Hoffman?"

"Yes," replied Mrs. Hoffman.

"I am Mr. Winter. I am going to be one

of the room parents on our trip to the museum today. Miss Mandel asked me to show you to her classroom. Are you ready to come with me?"

"We certainly are," said Mrs. Hoffman.

Two by two, my classmates and I hopped off of our wonderful bus. We lined up in a double row. Mr. Winter led us through the doors to the school. The hallway inside looked like the hallway in Stoneybrook Academy. It was lined with pictures and drawings. I saw a display case full of trophies. And then I saw a staircase. It went up and up and up. Park West School was not as wide as my school, but it was a lot taller.

Mr. Winter began climbing the staircase. We followed him to the second floor. (Addie's mom took Addie to an elevator.) On the way up, I looked out the window. All I could see were the buildings across the street.

Soon we were standing outside a door marked 23. A sign on the door read Miss

Mandel — Grade 2. Mr. Winter opened the door for us. And there was Miss Mandel.

"Welcome!" she said. "Come on in."

I felt excited and a little nervous, so I gripped Hannie's hand. I stepped through the doorway. I found myself in a room that looked a lot like our classroom, just a little smaller. Our pen pals were sitting at their desks. They were smiling at us. I looked for somebody with red hair. And there she was, in the third row.

"Hello, Maxie!" I called.

"Hello, pen pal!" she replied.

My friends and I greeted our pen pals. I saw that, just like when our pen pals had visited Stoneybrook Academy, two chairs were at each desk. This was so the pen pals could sit together.

I hurried to Maxie's desk, and sat next to her.

"Hello," I said again. "I brought you a present."

"Cool," said Maxie. "Thanks." Then she

added, "I brought you a present, too."

We opened our presents quickly. (Maxie gave me a package of markers.) Then Miss Mandel said, "Girls and boys from Stoneybrook, as you know, our class has been learning about dinosaurs, too. We would like to show you the projects and displays we have been making. So stay with your pen pals and walk quietly around our room. My students will tell you what they have been doing."

Maxie showed me around the room. And then . . . Miss Mandel took us on a tour of the school. We walked two by two again, but this time with our pen-pal partners. We started at the top of the school and worked our way down. Guess what. Maxie's school is *four* stories high. It does not have a gym. It has a *tiny* playground. For sports the kids mostly go to Central Park. For recess they go to the playground, or they can play in the *street*. During school hours, the street is blocked off. Cars cannot drive on it, so the kids can play there safely. Maxie's school has a kitchen, but no cafeteria. The kids eat in their classrooms.

When the tour was over, Miss Mandel led us back to her room. She looked at her watch. "Eleven o'clock," she said. "Who is ready to go to Central Park?"

"I am!" everyone shouted.

"Okay. Find your things, and let's go."

Central Park

My classmates and our pen pals and I gathered our things. Two by two we walked into the hallway, down the stairs, and through the door of Park West School. Then we set off for the park.

We did not have to walk far. We walked to a corner. A light at the crossing said DON'T WALK. So we waited. When it said WALK, we crossed the street. We walked to another corner. And guess what. We had almost reached the end of the street. Ahead of us was a low wall. Beyond it were lots of trees. I looked at a street sign. We had come to Central Park West again.

"There it is," said Maxie. "There is Central Park."

"Where?" I asked.

Maxie pointed ahead of us. "Right there."

"Where those trees are? That is the *park*? It is huge." The trees spread away from me to the left, to the right, and straight ahead as far as I could see.

"Yes," agreed Maxie. "It is quite huge."

"Do we climb over the wall?" I asked.

"Oh, no," said Maxie as we crossed the street and turned the corner. "We will go to a park entrance. It is just a few blocks away."

I glanced at Maxie. I wondered if she was bragging. She seemed to know an awful lot about the park. But Maxie did not seem to be bragging. In fact, she was peeking into her lunch bag.

"What did you bring?" I asked.

"Tomato and lettuce sandwich, a banana, and chips. And a juice box. What did you bring?"

"Peanut butter and jam sandwich, an apple, and carrot sticks. And a surprise. Part of the surprise is for you."

"Cool," said Maxie.

We turned into the park then, and all of a sudden — just like that — I did not feel as if I were in a city anymore. Of course, I could still hear horns honking. And I could still see skyscrapers. But I could also smell new grass and leaves and flowers. I could see flowers, too. And I could feel the coolness of the park.

We walked along a path and a road, and soon Mrs. Hoffman said, "Girls and boys, do you remember when Ms. Colman read *Stuart Little* to you?"

"Yes," we all cried.

"Well, here is the pond where Stuart has his adventure in the boat."

"*This* pond?" I cried. "This very pond?"

"This very pond," said Mrs. Hoffman.

"Excellent." I had loved the story about the mouse named Stuart.

We walked some more until Miss Mandel said, "Now we are going to see something about another wonderful book. Let me see if you can guess which book I mean. I am thinking of the Cheshire Cat and the Queen of Hearts and the White Rabbit and — "

"*Alice in Wonderland!*" Sara called out.

"Right," said Miss Mandel. "Look over there."

We looked where Miss Mandel was pointing and saw a big statue of Alice herself. Kids were climbing all over it. Grown-ups were taking their pictures. My friends and I ran to it, and we climbed on it, too.

Mrs. Hoffman and Miss Mandel let us play for awhile. Then Miss Mandel called, "Lunchtime!"

"Where are we going to eat?" I asked Maxie.

"Hmm. I am not sure. There are lots of good picnic spots," she replied.

So we walked along. We passed roller skaters and some people dancing and a man playing tin drums. Finally Miss Mandel said, "Here we are."

Picnic in the Park

We had reached a big grassy field. On the paths nearby I could see people on skates and bicycles and Rollerblades. Other people were walking their dogs or jogging. But the field was almost empty.

Miss Mandel and Mrs. Hoffman spread out some blankets and sheets. They let us sit wherever we wanted. Nancy and Hannie and I sat on a blanket with our pen pals. Nancy's pen pal is named Eli. Hannie's is named Jen.

Eli looked around at the rest of us. He

frowned. "Um, too many girls," he muttered. He stood up. "No offense, Nancy," he said. Then he hurried over to a blanketful of boys.

Nancy looked hurt. So I said, "All girls is better anyway."

"I guess," said Nancy. Then she glanced at the boys. They were holding a burping contest. She grinned. "I mean, definitely."

Nancy and Hannie and Maxie and Jen and I opened our lunches. We spread them out in front of us.

"Who wants to trade?" I asked. "I will trade anything." (Except for the lollipops. I had hidden those.)

"Me!" called Nancy and Hannie and Maxie and Jen.

Nancy traded her peanut butter and honey sandwich for Maxie's sandwich. I traded my apple for Jen's peach. Jen traded her crackers for Hannie's Fritos. Maxie traded her banana for Jen's Oreos. Hannie traded her bologna sandwich for my carrot sticks. Then Nancy changed her mind

about Maxie's sandwich and they traded back, and Maxie traded the sandwich for Jen's cheese slices. But I do not think Jen or anyone else really wanted that lettuce and tomato sandwich. It was very boring.

Our traded lunches were completely different from the ones we had started out with.

Jen crunched into the boring sandwich. She wrinkled her nose. "Ew. This is like a salad between slices of bread."

"Brachiosaurus would have liked it," said Nancy. "Brachiosaurus was a plant-eater. That's the dinosaur Eli and I chose."

"Jen and I chose triceratops," said Hannie.

"Karen and I chose ornitholestes," said Maxie.

"Triceratops looked like a big rhinoceros," said Jen.

"Ornitholestes means 'bird robber,'" I said.

"Brachiosaurus won burping contests," said Nancy, and we laughed.

I ate my sandwich and looked around the park. I saw a girl throwing a Frisbee to a dog. I saw a man holding a Discman and dancing on his Rollerblades. I saw a group of little kids taking a walk with their teacher.

I decided I loved Central Park. There was so much to see.

"You know," said Maxie, "millions and millions of years ago, dinosaurs might have lived right here."

"In Central Park?" exclaimed Hannie.

"Well, it was not Central Park then," said Maxie. "It was just land."

"Yeah," I said. "Maybe here in this very spot, ornistholestes went around stealing innocent little birds."

"Did ornistholestes really steal birds?" asked Jen.

"Well, the scientists think maybe ornistholestes *hunted* birds," I said.

My friends and I looked around. I knew we were all imagining the park as it might have been long ago, with dinosaurs roaming it. I shivered. The thought was deliciously scary.

We finished our lunches then. I gave Maxie her chocolate lollipop and bit into mine. We were just taking the last bites of them when Mrs. Hoffman said, "Okay, everybody. It is time to go to the museum."

"Yes!" I cried.

The Biggest Museum

My friends and I gathered up our trash. Miss Mandel showed us a litter can and we threw our garbage in it. Then the teachers folded up the sheets and blankets, and we kids picked up our backpacks and jackets and things.

"Pen-pal partners!" called Miss Mandel.

I grabbed Maxie's hand. Two by two we walked through the park again. I saw that we had returned to the big street called Central Park West. We walked along it until I heard Maxie say, "There it is."

This time she was pointing across the street to an enormous stone building. It was one of the biggest buildings I had ever seen. I knew it was the biggest museum I had ever seen. It was about a hundred times bigger than the art museum in Stoneybrook.

"It — it is huge!" I whispered.

"It has to be," replied Maxie. "Just think. An entire apatosaurus is in there. Plus other dinosaurs. And animals and collections and jewels and — and, well, a lot of other things."

Wide stone steps led up to the entrance to the American Museum of Natural History. In our two-by-two line we climbed them.

"We are really supposed to use a different entrance," I heard Miss Mandel say to Mrs. Hoffman. "But I want the kids to see the main entrance." (Addie and her mom and pen pal used another entrance, though, so Addie would not have to go up all those steps.)

A few moments later, I understood why Miss Mandel wanted us to see the main entrance. We had stepped into a large, dark, hushed room with high ceilings and tall, tall columns. I felt as if I were in a palace. I just looked and looked. I could not even say anything.

Miss Mandel spoke to a woman behind a desk. Then she joined the rest of us again. "Okay," she said. "Before we go to the dinosaur halls, we will take a quick tour of the museum. Most of the kids in Mrs. Hoffman's class have not been here before. My students have been here several times. But you do not mind walking through it again, do you?" (Miss Mandel was smiling.)

"No!" cried her students.

And Jen said, "Can we go see the gems and minerals?"

"And the meteorites?" asked Eli.

"The skeleton hologram?" asked Maxie.

"The poison dart frogs?" asked Jamal.

"Not real ones," Maxie whispered to me.

"Oh, good," I whispered back.

"Can we go to the gift shop?" asked Pamela.

"We will try to see as many things as we can," replied Miss Mandel.

"But we will not have time to go to any of the gift shops," added Mrs. Hoffman.

No gift shops? I thought. Boo and bull-frogs.

"All right, let's go," said Miss Mandel.

We walked through a room and soon I saw, far above my head . . . an enormous blue whale. The whale was a model. It was 94 feet long. We walked all around the first floor. We walked through an insect collection, and the minerals and gems collection, and the meteorite displays, and displays of birds and mammals and about Native Americans.

On the second floor we saw lots more birds and animals. (They were not alive — they were stuffed — but they looked very real.) We saw displays about Asian peoples and South American peoples and African peoples.

"I wish we could spend more time here," said Miss Mandel, "but we must hurry through. We must go to the dinosaur halls so you can begin your projects. I just want you to have a look at the museum."

On the third floor we saw birds, African mammals, primates, and reptiles and amphibians. We saw displays about more Native Americans.

At last Miss Mandel said, "Boys and girls, we are about to go to the fourth floor. That is where the dinosaur halls are. Is everybody ready?"

"Ready!" we said.

And we began to climb the stairs.

17

The Dinosaur Halls

Guess what we saw as soon as we had climbed to the fourth floor. Another museum gift shop. We had seen several in the museum, but Mrs. Hoffman and Miss Mandel had hurried us past each one.

"Mrs. Hoffman, can we just go to this gift shop? Puh-*lease*?" I asked. I could see dinosaur things inside. And I had a pocketful of spending money. I had been saving my allowance for weeks.

"Karen, I am sorry," said Mrs. Hoffman, "but we do not have time to go into the

84

stores. We truly do not. We have just enough time to work on our projects now. Then we will have to hurry to our bus. We have a long ride back to Stoneybrook."

Double boo and bullfrogs. I had thought Mrs. Hoffman might let some of us at least peek into the gift shop. But no. A few moments later, though, I forgot about the gift shop.

"Boys and girls," said Miss Mandel, "welcome to the Halls of the Dinosaurs. The saurischian dinosaurs are over here. The ornithischian dinosaurs are over there."

I peered into the Hall of the Saurischian Dinosaurs. I gasped. The very first thing I saw was a skeleton of apatosaurus. And it was not just a little model skeleton. It was the size of a real apatosaurus. It was 86 feet long. In display cases were fossils and bones and skeletons and skulls of other dinosaurs. I could not believe my eyes.

I wanted to look for ornitholestes right away, but Mrs. Hoffman said. "Let's take

a peek in the Hall of the Ornithischian Dinosaurs first. Then you can split up to work on your projects. I will stay with those of you working in this hall. Miss Mandel will stay with those of you working in the other hall."

So I followed Mrs. Hoffman into the other room. The first thing I saw there was the skeleton of a stegosaurus. It was only 20 feet long. But still, "Maxie!" I whispered loudly. "A stegosaurus." I counted the plates down the dinosaur's back. I looked at the spikes at the end of its tail. "The stegosaurus lived one hundred and forty *million* years ago," I said.

I could not believe my eyes. I decided the museum was one of the best places I had ever visited. I thought about David Michael. I knew he would think it was one of the best places *he* had ever visited, too. (I felt a little bad about that.)

"Time to begin your projects now," said Mrs. Hoffman.

Maxie and I went with Mrs. Hoffman to the other hall.

"I hope ornitholestes is here," I said to Maxie.

"Me, too," she agreed.

We began to look.

We checked every single display. And soon we found it.

"Look!" exclaimed Maxie. "A skeleton, a whole skeleton."

There was ornitholestes. Ornitholestes was just seven feet long, but that was okay. I loved its tail and its three-fingered front legs. Ornitholestes had also lived about 140 million years ago.

"Okay, let's start the poster of our dinosaur," I said.

Maxie laid out the piece of posterboard Mrs. Hoffman had given us. First we tried to draw a picture of ornitholestes. Then I carefully wrote WANTED.

"Wanted for what?" said Maxie thoughtfully.

"For bird stealing, of course," I replied.

So Maxie wrote "bird stealing." Then we wrote down ornitholestes's description: 7 feet long, small skull, long tail, pointed teeth, birdlike, can run very fast, meat-eating, may hunt birds or even baby dinosaurs, 140 million years old.

Very soon, Mrs. Hoffman collected our posters. "Miss Mandel will put up the posters in her room for awhile," she said. "Then she will send them to me, and I will put them up in our room."

I looked at the skeleton of ornitholestes one last time. I loved my dinosaur. I wished I could have lived in the time of the dinosaurs.

Lost

"Which dinosaur do you like best?" Maxie asked me as we left the dinosaur halls.

"Definitely ornitholestes," I replied. "It did not used to be my favorite, but now it is."

"Yeah. Our dinosaur," agreed Maxie.

"Our dinosaur," I repeated.

Mrs. Hoffman and Miss Mandel and the room parents and our pen pals and my classmates and I met outside the dinosaur halls.

"Time to go," said Mrs. Hoffman. She looked as if she were in a rush.

"I cannot believe we have to leave our dinosaur," I said to Maxie.

But we did. We walked along a hallway. We walked down a flight of stairs. "Let's take the elevators," suggested Miss Mandel.

So we turned a corner and I saw . . . another gift shop. More dinosaur things were inside. I thought of David Michael again. I thought about how mad he was that he could not come to the wonderful museum. If I could just buy a dinosaur for him in the shop, he would probably feel a lot better.

I looked at my classmates waiting for the elevator. I looked at Maxie. Suddenly I whispered, "I will be right back." Then I ducked into the gift shop. I peeked back outside. Good. No one had seen me leave (except Maxie). Everyone was still waiting for the elevators.

Maxie was looking at me, though. Her

face was a big question mark. I waved to her to say that everything was all right. Then I turned around.

What a wonderful gift shop. I just love gift shops. Once when I was on a trip with my little-house family we stopped at a place called the Trading Post. Inside were a snack bar and a gift shop. I bought beaded moccasins. And once at a gift shop at the beach I bought a stick of rock candy.

This gift shop did not have moccasins or rock candy. But it had books, some toys, and *lots* of dinosaur things. This was perfect. Maybe I could even find an ornitholestes for David Michael.

First I checked a shelf of model dinosaurs. I saw an apatosaurus, a stegosaurus, a diplodocus, a triceratops, and a styracosaurus. But no ornitholestes. I checked one of the price tags. "Twenty-six dollars!" I exclaimed. Even if ornitholestes had been there, I could not have bought one. I had four dollars and eighteen cents in my pocket. That was all.

I crossed to another part of the gift shop. I looked at a shelf of books about dinosaurs. Most of them were big and beautiful. They cost way more than four dollars. Finally I saw a teeny little paperback book. Inside was a whole page about ornitholestes. I checked the price. Four dollars and fifty cents.

Boo and bullfrogs.

I was about to give up when I saw a basketful of small rubber dinosaurs. A sign on the basket read $1.25 EACH.

Goody. A dollar and a quarter. I could buy *three* dinosaurs.

Before I looked through the basket, I peered out the door. My class was still waiting by the elevator. Maxie waved to me madly. And she mouthed something to me. I think she was saying, "Hurry!"

I held up my finger to say, "Just a minute."

Then I raced back to the basket. I pawed through it. I found a dinosaur that looked very much like ornitholestes. I pulled it out.

Then I pulled out a stegosaurus and an apatosaurus. I hurried to the cash register. Two people were ahead of me on line. I tried to look out the door and into the hallway to see what my classmates were doing. But I was too far away.

I waited on that line. I did not wait patiently. I tapped my feet.

Finally it was my turn. I reached up and put the dinosaurs on the counter. The man behind the register rang them up.

"Four dollars and six cents, please," he said.

Oops. I had forgotten about sales tax. Oh, well. At least I had enough money. And I had twelve cents left over.

I took the bag the man handed me. I ran into the hall.

My class was gone.

Ornitholestes to the Rescue

Maybe I was in the wrong hallway. I hurried into the gift shop again. I looked for another way out. Nope. I had come out of the door I had gone in. There was the elevator.

I thought about getting on the elevator and riding down myself. But I was not sure which floor to go to. I knew our bus was waiting somewhere outside. But there are museum entrances on the first floor and the floor below. Besides, Mrs. Hoffman had said, "If you get separated from the group, stay where you are." She had said that many times.

She had also said to look for a police officer or an adult you can trust. I did not really think I was going to find a police officer in the American Museum of Natural History, but you never know.

So I stood in the hallway and looked for a police officer. I waited for five minutes. No luck.

I began to feel nervous. What if Mrs. Hoffman and my classmates climbed on our bus and left for Stoneybrook without me? I would be stuck here in New York City. I did not even have a quarter to phone Maxie with. I had only twelve cents. Maybe I could sell one of the dinosaurs back to the man in the gift shop. Then I would have $1.47.

I waited for a few more minutes. I looked for someone who worked in the museum. I did not see anyone. I looked in the gift shop. Maybe I could tell the man at the cash register what had happened. But I did not see him, either.

I started to cry.

Then I stopped. I had thought of something important. Maxie would not let my bus leave without me. She would tell Mrs. Hoffman what had happened. She would know where to find me.

Wouldn't she? I wondered why no one had come back for me yet.

I waited for five *more* minutes.

Then I thought of something else. I had seen lots of gift shops in the museum. Maybe Maxie could not remember which one I had gone into. They all look sort of the same. And the museum is a very big place.

I began to cry again. I peered into the gift shop. Still I could not see the man who had helped me.

Now what? Where else would Maxie look for me?

Suddenly, I had the answer. I knew — I

just *knew* — that Maxie would think to look at our dinosaur. At ornitholestes. She might not know which shop I had gone to. But she could tell Mrs. Hoffman to go to ornitholestes. Mrs. Hoffman could find our dinosaur.

But could I? I remembered we had walked down a flight of stairs near the gift shop. I looked around. I saw the stairs. I climbed them to the next floor. I walked along until I saw the Hall of Ornithischian Dinosaurs. That was where ornitholestes would be. I peeped in the room. It was almost empty. I ran to our dinosaur.

I stood by ornitholestes and waited.

And waited and waited.

And after a little while I heard voices. I looked toward the doorway. I saw Maxie and Mrs. Hoffman. They were running to me.

"There she is!" cried Maxie.

"You were right!" exclaimed Mrs. Hoffman. "Karen did go back to your dinosaur. Oh, Karen, we were so worried about you!"

Mrs. Hoffman put her arms around me and gave me a hug.

"I told Mrs. Hoffman how you got *lost*," said Maxie. "You know, *lost*."

"Oh, *lost*," I repeated. Whew. Maxie had not told Mrs. Hoffman about the gift shop. That would be our secret. "I know I was supposed to stay in one place," I said. "But I waited and waited. And then I thought of my dinosaur. So I came here."

"You did the right thing, Karen," replied Mrs. Hoffman. "Now let's hurry. Everyone is waiting."

A Present for David Michael

Mrs. Hoffman and Maxie and I rode the elevator down, down, down. When the doors opened, I saw my classmates and our pen pals and Miss Mandel and the room parents.

It was time to say good-bye.

"Good-bye, Maxie," I said. "I will write you a letter soon. And thank you for not telling Mrs. Hoffman about the gift shop." I whispered. "I had to buy a present for my brother. It was *really* important. I will tell you why in the letter."

Maxie nodded. "Okay. I am glad we got to see each other again. Today was really fun. And don't worry. I will keep our secret."

"Class, come on!" called Mrs. Hoffman then.

"Good-bye! Good-bye!" said my classmates.

"Good-bye! Good-bye!" said our pen pals.

A few minutes later I was sitting on the wonderful bus with Hannie again.

"What shall we do first?" asked Hannie.

"Let's just look out the window," I answered. I was tired. (I could tell Hannie was, too.) So we looked at the lights in the apartment buildings and skyscrapers. Everything seemed to be lit up. As we left the city, I turned around. I looked at the lights behind me. Then I fell asleep.

I did not wake up until I heard Mrs. Hoffman say, "Rise and shine, everybody. We are home again."

I blinked. I yawned. I looked out the window. I saw more lights, but these were the lights of Stoneybrook. A few minutes later, we pulled into the parking lot of our school. My sleepy classmates stepped off the wonderful bus and found their parents.

Mrs. Papadakis drove Hannie and me home. By the time I reached the big house, I was wide awake. I felt quite peppy after my nap.

"Hello, everyone!" I yelled when I opened the front door.

"Karen, hello," said Daddy. "How was your trip?"

My big-house family was gathering in the kitchen.

"It was great!" I exclaimed. "We ate lunch in Central Park."

"Did you see Maxie?" asked Andrew.

"Oh, yes. I went to her school, and I saw her room and her desk. And Miss Mandel and all the other kids were there, of course."

"How did you get to the park?" asked Kristy.

"We walked. We walked to the park and all around inside it. Then after our picnic, we walked to the museum, too."

"How was the museum?" asked Elizabeth.

"It was so cool. It was *huge*. Can we go back there someday? Because there are tons of things we did not get to see. Like meteorites — "

"Meteorites?" said David Michael.

"Yes, and animal displays and — " I stopped. I did not want my brother to feel bad all over again about not going to the museum. "Anyway, Maxie and I found our dinosaur and we made the poster. We had lots of fun." (I did not mention that I had sort of gotten lost.)

I waited until dinner was over to give David Michael his present. I found him in his room. I think he was supposed to be doing his homework, but he was reading comic books.

"David Michael?" I said. "I bought something for you at the museum today. Ac-

tually, I bought three things for you." I put the dinosaurs on his bed. "See? This one is ornitholestes. Or it could be."

"Thanks," said David Michael.

"I am really sorry you did not get to go to the museum. You would have liked it. Maxie and I saw a skeleton of ornitholestes. Maybe Daddy and Elizabeth will take us back to the museum someday. Anyway, I am also sorry we had a fight. I hope you like the dinosaurs."

"Thanks," said David Michael again. "And I am sorry, too. I just got mad. But I am tired of fighting." David Michael looked at the dinosaurs. Then he handed one back to me. "Here. You can have apatosaurus. You should have a souvenir of your trip."

I took it from him. I grinned. "Thank *you*."

Our fight was over and the trip was over. It had been a long day. But I was very, very happy.

About the Author

ANN M. MARTIN lives in New York City and loves animals, especially cats. She has two cats of her own, Gussie and Woody.

Other books by Ann M. Martin that you might enjoy are *Stage Fright*; *Me and Katie (the Pest)*; and the books in *The Baby-sitters Club* series.

Ann likes ice cream and *I Love Lucy*. And she has her own little sister, whose name is Jane.

BABY-SITTERS
Little Sister

Don't miss #74

KAREN'S SOFTBALL MYSTERY

More things were stolen at practice on Tuesday: two bats, another left-hand catcher's mitt, another right-hand batting glove. On Wednesday, Kristy's notebook disappeared for awhile. When it turned up again, something mysterious had happened to it.

"I don't get it. Someone erased my statistics and wrote in phony numbers," said Kristy.

Who was doing these mysterious things? And why? This was a case for serious detectives. It was a case for the Three Musketeers!

I called Hannie and Nancy over for a meeting.

"We have a real mystery here," I said. "If we do not solve the case soon, the Krushers could be ruined for the season."

LITTLE APPLE®

BABY SITTERS Little Sister™

by Ann M. Martin,
author of The Baby-sitters Club®

More Titles... ➡